LITTLE GIRL WITH SEVEN NAMES

by Mabel Leigh Hunt

Illustrated by Grace Paull

Her uncle Mark was the only one in the family who called the little Quaker girl by her full name and he always made a huge joke of it. It wasn't fun, though, when the first day of school she had to stand up and tell her full name. The children laughed, because it was Melissa Louisa Amanda Miranda Cynthia Jane Farlow. Seven names! Since she was the first girl in the family, she was named after her two grandmothers and four aunts, so no one would be hurt. She kept wishing she could get rid of at least two of her names, but she didn't know how nor which ones to give up. Her problem was solved in the most wonderful way.

Classification and Dewey Decimal: Fiction (Fic)

About the Author:

Librarian and author MABEL LEIGH HUNT spent her early life in a college town in Indiana, in the environment of books and people who liked books. She worked as a librarian and finds writing children's books a delightful and rewarding occupation.

About the Illustrator:

GRACE PAULL, author and illustrator, studied at Pratt Institute and Art Students League in New York. Her interests have included flower gardening, lithography and water coloring. Museums and galleries have exhibited her works. Miss Paull lives in Cold Brook, New York.

LITTLE GIRL WITH SEVEN NAMES

LITTLE GIRL WITH SEVEN NAMES

BY

MABEL LEIGH HUNT

Illustrated by GRACE PAULL

1968 FIRST CADMUS EDITION
THIS SPECIAL EDITION IS PUBLISHED BY ARRANGEMENT WITH
THE PUBLISHERS OF THE REGULAR EDITION
J. B. LIPPINCOTT COMPANY
BY
E. M. HALE AND COMPANY
EAU CLAIRE, WISCONSIN

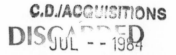

Library of Congress Catalog Card Number 36-20142

This edition lithographed in U.S.A. by Wetzel Brothers, Inc., Milwaukee, Wisconsin

To

My Small Kinswoman

ROSEMARY WRIGHT

aged eight

CHAPTER I

There was once a little girl who had a name as long as that of any royal princess.

But she was not a princess.

She was just a little Quaker girl who lived with her father and mother on an American farm. There were freckles on her nose. A fat little, tight little braid peeped out from behind each ear. Pantalettes, as white as snow, twinkled below the hem of her skirts. And her eyes were the same color as the bluebells that bloomed in the wood just down the road.

As for her name, truly there were so many words in it that only one person ever called her by all of them. That was her Uncle Mark. And he did it just to tease.

When Uncle Mark came to the farmhouse, his little niece always ran to the door to greet him. For she loved him very much, and she thought that surely there could be no other uncle in all the world half so jolly.

And the moment that Uncle Mark clapped eyes on her, he would begin to behave in the strangest manner.

First he would work his arms up and down, limbering up his muscles. He would teeter up and down on his toes, too. Then he would take a very long, deep breath, as if he were getting ready to run a race. He would hold the breath in his mouth until both his big cheeks puffed out like round, red apples.

Then suddenly his cheeks would cave in, with a noise like *P-p-w-u-h!* His mouth would burst open, and out would come tumbling, so fast that all the names seemed to run together into one, the words that had made Uncle Mark's cheeks as fat as round, red apples.

2

"Good-day-to-thee, Melissa-Louisa-Amanda-Miranda-Cynthia-Jane-Farlow!"

Then he would sigh, fanning himself with his hat, and sink down into the nearest chair. Or he would stagger up against the wall, breathing hard, pretending to be completely worn out with all the work of saying Melissa Louisa's long, long name.

She would run to him with a drink of water, or of sweet cider. He would throw back his head,

3

and swallow the drink in one huge gulp, and clear his throat, and slap his chest.

Then he and Melissa Louisa would burst out laughing. They would laugh and laugh and laugh! The joke was always the same. Yet neither one of them ever grew tired of it.

So that Melissa Louisa Amanda Miranda Cynthia Jane Farlow thought it was great fun to have such a long, long name.

John and Mary Farlow, who were the parents of this little Quaker maid, called her only Melissa Louisa. That was quite enough of a name for everyday use. For how funny it would have been—now wouldn't it?—for them to have said, "Blow thy nose, Melissa Louisa Amanda Miranda Cynthia Jane Farlow." Or, "Melissa Louisa Amanda Miranda Cynthia Jane Farlow, thee may feed the chickens."

But when she was born, they had given her all these names for a very special reason. For they had said, "Since this is the first little girl in the family,

4

we shall name her for her two grandmothers and her four aunts. Then no one's feelings will be hurt, and everyone will be happy."

The two grandmothers and the four aunts were indeed very happy to have the new baby named for them. As she grew up, each one of them, and Uncle Mark, too, secretly thought that there was no child in all the world so dear as Melissa Louisa Amanda Miranda Cynthia Jane Farlow. But they were very careful not to show their love for her out-and-out, for they weren't going to have a child in *their* family with spoiled and unseemly manners.

So that in spite of having a father and a mother and two grandmothers and four aunts and an uncle and no brothers and sisters, nor even any cousins, Melissa Louisa was really quite a good little person.

CHAPTER II

It was from Grandmother Melissa Gray that Melissa Louisa got her first name.

Grandmother Gray was one of the dearest grandmothers a little girl ever had. You had to go around the bend of the road, through the covered bridge, past a crossroads, and over two hills before you reached Grandmother Gray's house. So that Melissa Louisa did not see her as often as she would have liked.

But on First Days, when everyone went to Meeting in the little white meeting-house, Grandmother Gray always managed to sit next to Melissa Louisa. She would hold the little girl's hand in her gentle warm one, and Melissa Louisa would lean

her head against Grandmother Gray's soft silken shoulder, and sit as quietly as a mouse, even though her feet sometimes went to sleep.

And every First Day, during Meeting, when it was so still that one could have heard a pin drop, the little girl would begin to wonder what surprise lay hidden this time in the pocket of Grandmother Gray's full skirt. Although she tried with all her might not to think about it, and to send little pray-

7

ers to the Lord, asking Him to help her to be a better girl, it just seemed that she couldn't ever keep from thinking of Grandmother's pocket.

So that by the time Meeting was over, and everyone was shaking hands, and greeting each other, Melissa Louisa was as hungry as a little bear. But she kept it to herself, and never said a word, for she had been taught to be mannerly.

Then Grandmother Gray would fumble among the folds of her silken skirt, until she found her pocket. And out would come a big brown cooky, or a stick of hoarhound candy, or a peppermint drop. She would hold out the sweet to Melissa Louisa and say, "This will stay thy hunger until thee gets thy dinner, Melissa."

She never bothered about any of the child's other names. The one name of *Melissa* was quite enough for Grandmother Melissa Gray.

Melissa Louisa got her second name from Grandmother Louisa Farlow.

She was a dear grandmother, too, but very different from Grandmother Gray. Her farm adjoined Melissa Louisa's father's farm, so that she lived only a short distance down the road, and Melissa Louisa saw her often. Grandmother Farlow thought that everyone should be good ALL of the time! And no matter how often she saw Melissa Louisa, she would say, "And has thee been a good girl, Louisa-child?"

Grandmother Louisa Farlow never called Melissa Louisa by any other name than *Louisa*.

Aunt Amanda and Aunt Miranda were twins. They lived with Grandmother Gray, for they were her daughters. Melissa Louisa loved them very much. They were slim and pretty, and cared a great deal how they looked when they went to Meeting, or to make calls.

Grandmother Farlow said that "it would be more seemly if Amanda and Miranda Gray spent less time stitching tucks into their petticoats, and more time preparing their souls for the hereafter."

But Melissa Louisa could not help feeling proud of her twin aunts when she saw how very sweet they looked in their dainty sprigged delaines or calicoes, and she thought that their curls peeped out from under their plain little bonnets in the prettiest way imaginable.

It was impossible to tell them apart, for they were as like as two sweet-pea blossoms. So that when Melissa Louisa saw Aunt Amanda, she would say, "Good day to thee, Aunt Amanda-Miranda."

And when she saw Aunt Miranda she would say, "Good day to thee, Aunt Amanda-Miranda."

For that was perfectly safe, as one of them was bound to be either Aunt Amanda or Aunt Miranda.

The dimples would dance in the pink cheeks of the twin aunts, and they would say, "Good day to *thee*, little Amanda Miranda."

It was nice to be named for two such charming aunts. Melissa Louisa wished that she had inherited their curls as well as their names.

Aunt Cynthia and Aunt Jane were Father's sisters, and they lived with Grandmother Farlow in the farmhouse just down the road.

Aunt Cynthia was tall and thin. She was very, very good. She was very, very serious. And she spent a great deal of time teaching Melissa Louisa how to sew, how to be mannerly and, above all, how to be GOOD.

For she said, "First thee must please the Lord. But I want my little namesake to be a credit to me, too."

Aunt Jane was short and stout, and very sensible. She liked to milk, and take care of the chickens and the baby animals on the farm. She could make the best butter and cheese of any woman in the countryside. She was also what people called "a natural-born nurse," so that she was away from home a great deal of the time, taking care of sick people.

Aunt Jane said, "Between thee and me, child, the name of *Jane* would have been quite enough for thee. It would have suited thee, too. There aren't any fol-de-rols about *Jane*."

Melissa Louisa often wondered if she could ever be as good as Aunt Cynthia. Or as useful as Aunt Jane. She thought it a great honor to be named for them. But sometimes she felt a little worried for fear she would not grow up to be a credit to them.

All of which explains how Melissa Louisa Amanda Miranda Cynthia Jane Farlow happened to have so many names. Seven names she had—and she thought it was very nice until her first day at school.

13

CHAPTER III

Melissa Louisa had been looking forward to going to school for a long time. She could scarcely wait for the day to come.

But at last one morning her hair was brushed extra smooth, and pulled back into extra tight braids. She put on her starchy pink-and-white checkered pinafore. She took her new slate under her arm, and her lunch-basket in her hand. She gave her mother a quick little kiss. Her father took her up behind him on his horse. They rode off to the schoolhouse, and he left her at the door.

She was scarcely a bit afraid. For Aunt Cynthia, in teaching her to be mannerly, had always said, "Thee must ever remember, dear child, that it is almost as rude to be too shy as to be over-bold.

14

Therefore thee must always speak when thee is spoken to."

And then there was Anna Hadley, a nice big girl, who came and took her hand, and began at once to look after her.

Melissa Louisa felt very proud to be sitting there in the school-room, along with all the other new scholars, and with the older children, who had been going to school for a long time. Away in the back of the room there were boys almost as tall as her father. For in the little country schools of long ago, everyone, large and small, sat together in the one room.

Melissa Louisa thought that these big boys and girls must have learned a great deal at school. But she said to herself that it would not be long until she had learned a great deal, too.

There was a new teacher. He stood up very tall by his desk, and read a chapter from the Bible. Then he said, "We shall now call the roll." And he took up his quill pen, and made ready to write down the names of all the children. "Each scholar," said the teacher, "must stand up, in turn, and give his or her full name."

The teacher began with the biggest boy, away over in the opposite corner from where Melissa Louisa sat. The children stood up by their desks, one by one, and told their names.

There was one girl who was shy of the new teacher. When it came her turn to tell her name, she hung her head and whispered, "Mary Ann." The teacher rapped on his desk quite crossly, and said in a loud tone, "Thy full name, please." The girl blushed, and hung her head a little lower, and said, in a voice that one could scarcely hear, "Scott." The teacher said, "It took thee a long time, Mary Ann Scott, to tell thy full name."

After that, the children knew for certain that the teacher would be cross if he was not promptly told every single name that one owned.

Each of the children had two names, of course. Some had three names. One boy had four names. When it came his turn, he rattled off, "Elbert Elijah Elihu Edwards."

But no one had seven names, as Melissa Louisa had, and underneath her checkered pinafore her heart began to beat like a little trip-hammer, as the time drew nearer and nearer for her to stand up and tell her full name.

17

At last the teacher looked straight at her.

Aunt Cynthia, and indeed all of the four aunts and the two grandmothers, and Uncle Mark, as well, would have been pleased could they have seen how bravely she stood up, and in what a clear, proud little voice she recited her name.

"Melissa Louisa Amanda Miranda Cynthia Jane Farlow," she said.

The teacher's eyes widened in surprise. His eyebrows went up. And at that all of the scholars laughed! Some of them giggled, and some of them, especially the big boys, simply shouted!

For a moment Melissa Louisa didn't know what had happened. Had one of her braids turned into a fire-cracker, and exploded just behind her ear, she could not have been more surprised.

Slowly she sank into her seat, her face and neck growing pinker and pinker until she was as pink as her pink pinafore.

The whole school had laughed at her!

And suddenly she wanted to cry, and run

home to her mother, and never, never come back to school again. Oh, dear—oh, dear! To think how long she had been wanting to start to school, and now it wasn't nice after all! It was horrid!

The new teacher saw the tears in Melissa Louisa's eyes.

He rapped on his desk. "Silence!" he thundered, and he looked sternly at all of the children. "There is no reason for laughing," he said. "This child was given a name by her parents, and who are you to question the wisdom of your elders?"

He paused, and looked down at the ledger, where he had written Melissa Louisa's full name. "Seven names," said the teacher, "are no more funny than two. And that is not funny at all."

"Now, child," he said, looking kindly down at Melissa Louisa, "by what name is thee called at home?"

There was such a big lump in Melissa Louisa's throat that she could not speak.

Anna Hadley came to the rescue. She raised

her hand. "Please, Teacher," she said, "they call her Melissa Louisa."

"Very well," said the teacher. "Next," and he called on the child who sat behind Melissa Louisa.

At recess a hateful boy called over from the boys' side of the playground, "Hello, thee little Melissa Louisa Amanda Miranda Cynthy Jane Mary Patty Polly Susan Rebecca!"

"Never thee mind, honey," said Anna Hadley. "See what I'm doing!"

Melissa Louisa looked up at Anna. She was wrinkling up her nose, making an ugly face at the bad boy. Her tongue stuck away out.

It made Melissa Louisa laugh. She stuck out her tongue, too, but it only came out a tiny bit. Because she happened to remember, just in time, what Grandmother Farlow and Aunt Cynthia would have thought if they could have seen her sticking out her tongue at anybody.

But she felt better, and she skipped into the schoolhouse, holding tight to Anna Hadley's hand.

20

At home that evening, Mother and Father wanted to know how their little daughter liked school. "I didn't like it much," she said, in a small voice. But she was ashamed to tell what had happened to cause her so much disappointment.

The next time that Uncle Mark came, Melissa Louisa laughed with him again over her name, and *pretended* to think that his "monkey-shines" were just as funny as ever. For Aunt Cynthia had taught her to be kind and polite, and she thought that Uncle Mark would be hurt if she did not laugh as usual. But it was only her face that laughed, and not her heart.

Uncle Mark's joke never again seemed very funny to Melissa Louisa. Never after the day the children laughed at her long, long name.

But of course she had to go to school, whether she liked it or not.

Melissa Louisa thought a great deal about it all. She wished that Father and Mother had not named her for so many people. And she wished that there was someone to whom she might give at least two of her names. Just giving one away would not make enough difference.

But it would never, never do to hurt the feelings of her two grandmothers and her four aunts. Moreover, how could a person give away such a fastened-on thing as a name? It would be almost like giving away one of her braids.

22

CHAPTER IV

Melissa Louisa had a doll named Ida.

She had a cat named John Doe.

She was very fond of both of them. But sometimes she felt as if she must shake Ida, because she would never answer, although Melissa Louisa talked to her by the hour, and she was quite sure that the doll heard every word she said.

When she complained about it to Uncle Mark, he said, "It does seem as if Ida will never be a chatterbox. She's a doll of few words, there's no doubt about that. But thee must remember she is a Quaker doll, and Quakers are given to meditation." Melissa Louisa knew all about what *that* meant, and she felt more patient with Ida, for there was no telling what deep thoughts were going on in her child's head.

John Doe, the cat, was a fellow who did just as he pleased. When he wanted to be fed, or petted, he would rub his smooth, furry cheek against Melissa Louisa's ankle, and he would purr as loud as could be, with his tail high over his back, oh, so friendly!

Or when he wanted to be lazy, he would lie soft and limp and cuddly in his mistress' lap.

But let him take a sudden notion, and down he would jump! He would stretch himself, and sharpen his claws on the door-step. Then off he would go on some secret errand of his own, and no amount of coaxing would bring him back until he was good-and-ready.

Melissa Louisa often said to herself, "If I only had a twin, like Aunt Amanda and Aunt Miranda!" For if she had a twin to play with, she would not have to depend altogether on Ida and John Doe for her fun.

There were no children living near. On one side of her father's farm there was Grandmother Farlow's farm. And on the other side there was Daniel and Susan Wheeler, a young married couple who had no children.

So that Melissa Louisa was sometimes a bit lonely. And since it was now too late to be a twin, she always remembered, when she sat in Meeting, or when she said her prayers at night, to ask the Lord to send her a baby brother or a baby sister.

For there was nothing in the world that Melissa Louisa admired as much as babies. She loved them much better than dolls, or cats. In fact, she liked them better than she did children her own age, and

when she went to make calls with her mother, if there was a baby in the house, she paid very little attention to the older brothers and sisters. She would kneel before this tiny one, hiding her face behind her hands to make the baby laugh. Or she would let it pull her braids, or pound her with its chubby fists. Sometimes she would be allowed to hold it carefully on her lap.

Her mother said, "Melissa Louisa seems to have a real *knack* with babies. She's just that much like her Aunt Jane."

One day Melissa Louisa's father came into the

house. There was a wide smile on his face. "I was just talking to Dan Wheeler down by the pasture fence," he said, "and thee can't guess, Melissa Louisa, what came to their house last night."

Melissa Louisa ran over and stood at her father's knee. "Was it a little baby calf?" she asked.

"No," said Father.

"Was it a little baby colt?"

"No. Something better than a baby colt. Much, much better."

"Oh, Father!" cried Melissa Louisa, and her eyes began to shine like stars. "Was it a real little baby?"

"Yes," said Father, "it was a real little baby."

"May we go and see it?" asked Melissa Louisa, and she began to hop around on one foot.

"Yes," said Father, "Dan said for thee and thy mother to come over tomorrow and see the new baby."

Melissa Louisa thought that she could never wait for tomorrow to come. She went to bed extra early so that the next day would come more quickly.

She lay there thinking what fun it would be to have a baby living just down the road.

"I wonder what they will name it," she said to herself.

And suddenly such a surprising thought came to her that she jumped right out of bed, and stood in the middle of the room in her little nightgown. The new thought caused her heart to beat as hard as if she had been running. "Goodness gracious *ever!*" whispered Melissa Louisa, and she gave a hop and a skip and a jump into a little patch of moonlight that fell through the window.

But presently she climbed slowly into her bed again, for she thought that this was something that she had better keep to herself.

"Yes, I shall ask Susan Wheeler if I may give the new baby two of my names," she whispered to Ida, who shared her pillow. "I shall ask her tomorrow, when I go over there."

"But which ones shall I give away? I can't give away *Melissa* or *Louisa*, because they belong to me

28

truly-truly. They belong to me more than any of my other names. And besides, it would never do to hurt the feelings of dear Grandmother Melissa Gray, or of dear Grandmother Louisa Farlow. And that would surely happen if I gave away *Melissa Louisa*."

But Ida was not a bit of help. Perhaps she knew, in her quiet little head, that it is seldom wise to give advice, for she never said a word. So Melissa Louisa had to do all the thinking for herself.

"*Amanda Miranda*. Oh, dear, they are the prettiest names I have! Why, they're almost like poetry!"

Amanda

Miranda.

Yes, they made a tiny, perfect poem.

"Look here, Ida," whispered Melissa Louisa, "if thee had a little poem in thy name, could thee bear to give it away to a perfect stranger? I just know thee couldn't!"

The names she gave away would have to be

29

Cynthia Jane, then. She began to think of herself without them, and how she would stand up at school next fall and say that now her name had only five words in it, instead of seven. Surely no one would laugh at her then!

"Melissa Louisa Amanda Miranda—Farlow," she whispered, and for a moment she felt almost as queer as if someone had cut off one of her braids.

But what would Aunt Cynthia think?

What would Aunt Jane think?

Melissa Louisa tossed and turned on her little bed.

"I know! I shall make Aunt Cynthia the very nicest sampler I can make, to let her know that I love her just as much as ever."

Into the sampler she would set her very neatest stitches, those same neat stitches that Aunt Cynthia had taught her to make. Her A B C's would march along as straight as soldiers. "And I shall make a basket full of apples, red and pink and blue. And all around the sampler there will run a little green vine, for a border." How many, many stitches it would take to make that border! But when it was finished, it would look as if the little green vine had grown around the sampler with magic speed, and caught its own little green tail in its own little green mouth.

"Now what shall I say on the sampler?"

Into Melissa Louisa's head popped the words that she would stitch into the sampler—the beautiful sampler that was to be a peace-offering to Aunt Cynthia.

"The Lord loveth a cheerful giver."

That would be just right! Melissa Louisa sighed with happiness to think it was all settled so nicely.

Now what could she do for Aunt Jane? Melissa Louisa stretched and yawned and rubbed her eyes. Before she could decide anything more, she had fallen fast asleep.

CHAPTER V

The next day was Saturday. There was no
school. A light snow lay on the ground. Melissa
Louisa and her mother put on their warmest wraps.
They walked down the road, past the wood, and in
at the front gate of the Wheeler place, where the
new baby had come to live.

The baby was tiny and red and wrinkled. When Melissa Louisa touched its velvety cheek ever so gently with her finger, it squirmed and made a funny face. But she thought it was as dear as could be, and at once she loved it with all her heart.

Now was the time! Her heart beat a little faster. She looked straight at Susan Wheeler, and said, "What was thee going to name her?"

"Her!" echoed Susan, and she laughed. "It's a boy, Melissa Louisa."

A BOY! Melissa Louisa's heart sank. After all her careful plans last night! *Cynthia Jane* would never do for a boy, of course. Oh, dear, she would have to keep her seven names all her life! She would always have to be Melissa Louisa Amanda Miranda Cynthia Jane Farlow! For a moment she was so disappointed that she wanted to cry. Only of course crying did no good.

"We're going to call the baby Tobiah for Dan's father," said Susan. "And thee must come over and see him often, Melissa Louisa. When he gets a little

33

older, thee can play with him, and help me take care of him."

"May I really and truly help?" asked Melissa Louisa, her eyes shining.

"Of course thee may," answered Susan.

After that, Ida grew more quiet than ever, for there was no one to talk to her. What with school, and the new little one at the Wheeler's, it seemed as if Melissa Louisa was away from home a great deal of the time. Poor Ida sat in the same position in a corner of the sofa for days and days.

And John Doe, in spite of being such an independent fellow, sometimes went mewing about the house, lonesome for Melissa Louisa.

For nearly every day, especially as spring came on, she stopped after school to see little Tobiah Wheeler. And when summer came, and there was no school, she went more and more often to play with him.

They called him Toby for short, and as he grew fatter and fatter, they sometimes called him Toby Jug.

Toby was always glad to see Melissa Louisa. And she really did help very much in taking care of him, so that Toby's mother was just as glad to see her little neighbor as Toby was. For she was a farmer's wife, and had a great deal to keep her busy.

"I declare, child," said Susan Wheeler, "I don't know what the baby and I would do without thee. Thee is a regular little mother—that's what thee is! Toby thinks as much of thee as he does of me, I do believe. I guess I'll just have to give him to thee."

Melissa Louisa's mouth fell open. "Give him to me! Thee means for keeps, Susan?"

Susan laughed. "Thee will just have to take Toby home with thee some day, and have him for thy baby. I reckon thee'd like that, wouldn't thee?"

Melissa Louisa laughed, too, for sheer joy. "Oh-h, thee knows I would, Susan!"

She squeezed Toby Jug so hard that he squealed and grabbed one of her braids. He pulled and pulled, until she squealed, too, and had to pry her braid out of his tight, fat fist.

When it came time to go home, Melissa Louisa said, "May I take Toby home with me now, Susan?"

"We-ell, perhaps not this time, honey. Perhaps thee'd better ask thy mother first," and Susan laughed again. "Maybe thy mother wouldn't want to bother with such a fat rascal as Toby Jug."

Melissa Louisa's small Quaker feet danced all the way home. To have dear little Toby Jug for her very own!

But she wouldn't tell Mother. It would be such

a lovely surprise. She felt very sure that Mother would be delighted to have Toby come and live with them. For now vacation was about over. Soon school would begin again, and Toby would be such company for Mother, for he was almost seven months old now, and he could say "Mum-mum," which meant "Mother."

No, Melissa Louisa would keep this exciting surprise until the time came when she actually carried Toby into the house, to keep for her very own.

CHAPTER VI

The next time that Melissa Louisa went to see Toby his mother said, "Oh, Melissa Louisa, I'm so glad that thee is here! I want to go up into the hill pasture and pick the blackberries. They will go to waste if I don't gather them soon. Will thee take care of Toby while I am gone? I shall be back in a couple of hours, I think."

Melissa Louisa felt very proud at the thought of being left in sole charge of the baby. Just like a grown-up! She listened carefully to all of Susan's directions, and she and Toby waved farewell from the kitchen door.

Susan had been gone only a little while when Melissa Louisa began to feel a bit lonesome. Just the wee-est bit scared in the quiet house, even with

Toby there. The very chairs and tables seemed suddenly to be full of strange secrets. The slow *tick-
tock* of the grandfather clock was louder than she
had ever heard it. Her eyes grew bigger and bigger,
and she wished that she were at home with ber own

mother. And there was Toby, with his mouth crumpling up, as if he were going to cry, if only he had reason enough.

All at once Melissa Louisa said to herself, "Now would be a good time to take Toby home with me, for keeps." And at once she felt as happy as a bird.

Yes, the time had come to give Mother the great surprise. Melissa Louisa's eyes danced as she thought how pleased Mother would be to have a real live baby in the house.

Susan would be surprised, too, when she returned from berry-picking, and found Toby gone. But Susan was so busy with the farm work and the baby to care for. How glad she would be to have him looked after and loved by her good neighbors! Besides, hadn't Susan as good as promised that she, Melissa Louisa, might carry Toby home with her one day?

"Does thee want to go abroady, darling Toby Jug?" she asked.

The baby held up his arms, and crowed.

40

Melissa Louisa began to gather up a few of his belongings. She could come back tomorrow and get all of his things.

Then she picked him up, and went out of the house, closing the door carefully behind her.

Melissa Louisa walked down the dusty road, carrying the baby. Quite often she had to set him

down on the grass and rest herself, for he was as fat as butter, and seemed to grow heavier with every step she took. It was very hot, and it seemed to her as if she would never reach home.

Toby had a wonderful time. He had not been out in the world many times, and this was a great treat for him. He pointed, with his funny, fat finger. He talked, in his funny baby language. He jumped up and down in Melissa Louisa's arms until she was afraid that she would drop him.

When they came to the wood, she decided that she must stop here in the shade until she was really rested.

Toby liked that, too. He crept about in the grass there by the roadside, picking up bits of twigs or tiny pebbles, holding them up proudly for Melissa Louisa to see.

Presently, like John Doe in his friendly moments, Toby climbed into Melissa Louisa's lap. In just a moment he had fallen asleep.

Melissa Louisa was tired enough to sleep, too.

42

But she struggled to her feet, and set forth again. This time Toby was as heavy as lead.

At last she reached home. It was hard to go tip-toeing into the house with such a heavy load in her arms. But tiptoe she did, so that the surprise would be more sudden for Mother.

But Mother was nowhere to be seen. Melissa Louisa guessed that she must be in the hen-house, or out in the barn, gathering the eggs. Very well, she would carry the sleeping baby into her own room. She would put him down on her own soft little bed. She would keep Toby's coming a secret until he woke up. She giggled a little to think how surprised dear Mother would be when she saw Toby, all rosy and fresh after his nap.

Melissa Louisa's room was dark and cool and quiet. She put Toby down in the middle of her bed. My, what a relief! How tired she was! Her arms were quite numb. But how comfortable Toby looked! Melissa Louisa's mouth opened in a wide, pink yawn. Why not lie down beside him and rest herself? Then, when Toby awakened in a strange room he would not be frightened. She climbed up on the bed.

There they lay, she and Toby, fast asleep.

The next thing that she knew was the sound of her mother's voice, calling her to supper. She sat up. There was Mother standing in the doorway.

"My, but that was a long nap!" said Mother. "I guess thee was completely tuckered out carrying the baby all that distance through the heat."

Mother knew about the surprise, then. What a shame she had been asleep when Mother discovered Toby! She looked down at the bed.

Toby was not there.

"Wasn't thee surprised, Mother?" she asked, and the dimples twinkled in her cheeks. "Where's Toby now?"

"His mother came and got him about an hour ago," answered Mother. "You were both asleep here together. Susan didn't know what to think when she came back from berry-picking and found

Toby gone. Thee should not have frightened her that way, child."

Melissa Louisa stared. "Susan came and took the baby away? Why, Mother, he's *mine!* Susan said that I could have him, Mother!"

"She was just joking, child, of course. No mother is going to give her baby away to anybody. Come to supper now."

But Melissa Louisa wouldn't come to supper. She flung herself face down on the bed. She sobbed as if her heart would break.

"S-S-Susan said that I c-c-could have him for k-k-keeps," she wailed. "And, oh-h-h, it was to b-be such a g-g-good surprise for thee, Mother. Oh—oh-h-h!"

It took Father and Mother both a long time to quiet their little daughter. They had to explain over and over that Susan was just teasing when she said that Melissa Louisa could have Toby for her very own. They told her that mothers loved their own babies better than anything in the world. They

45

said that it would be very strange, nay, downright wicked of Susan, to give her baby away, even to Melissa Louisa, who loved him so much.

"Just think," they said, "how very, very lonely Daniel and Susan would be without dear little Toby Jug!"

At last Melissa Louisa stopped crying.

46

Her mother bathed her reddened eyelids, and her swollen nose. She washed the dirty streaks off her cheeks where the tears had run down. She brushed her tumbled hair, and they all sat down to supper.

Uncle Mark came in while they were at the table. For once he did not play his joke about Melissa Louisa's name.

For although he was very polite, and pretended not to notice, he could see by his niece's red eyes and swollen nose, that she had been crying, and that she was in no mood for jokes of any kind whatsoever.

After supper he took her for a fast gallop on his horse. They rode a long way. At last they came to a crossroads store.

Uncle Mark got off his horse, and tied it to a post. He went into the store. And in no time at all he was back again. In two fingers he held a little sugar dove. It was as white and sparkling as hoar frost. It was really almost too pretty to eat.

"This is for a little girl who has a father and a

47

mother and two grandmothers and four aunts and
a *nuncle!*" said Uncle Mark.

"That's me," said Melissa Louisa, and she gave
the sugar dove a tiny lick with her tongue.

She felt much, much better.

CHAPTER VII

"Well, Melissa Louisa," said Father one morning, "does thee know that school begins in three days?"

"Will there be the same teacher as last year, Father?"

"No, he's going to teach over in town," answered Father. "So there will be a new teacher again this year."

"Oh, dear," thought Melissa Louisa to herself, "the new teacher will have us stand up and say our full names, and all the scholars will laugh at mine, like they did last year.

"Father, I don't believe I want to go to school this year," she said. "Couldn't I just stay at home with thee and Mother all the time?"

"And grow up to be a know-nothing?" cried Father. He looked horrified at the very thought. "Of course thee must go to school. Thee'll like it better this year, I'll just warrant.

"And I'll tell thee what, Daughter—thee's going to have a treat before thee starts to school. Daniel Wheeler's little niece is visiting over there, and they want thee to come over just as soon as thee can get ready, and stay all day, and all night to-night!"

Melissa Louisa had never stayed away from home all night before. She thought it would be fun to go, to play with Toby and Mary Wheeler, and to share Mary's bed at night.

So she put on a clean dress. She tucked her little nightgown and Ida under her arm. She kissed her mother good-bye, and set off for the visit, as happy as could be.

And she did have such a good time that she almost forgot her dread of starting to school. Toby had never been so cunning, and Mary was a very

nice little girl, with just the kind of curls that Melissa Louisa most admired. She was scarcely a bit
homesick when bedtime came, and she and Mary
went to sleep right in the middle of a spell of giggles.
She was sorry to say farewell when Father came on
horseback the next day to take her home again.

"There is a surprise awaiting thee at home,
Daughter," said Father, as they rode along.

"Oh! What is it?" cried Melissa Louisa, and
she hugged her father around the waist as tight as
she could.

"It won't be a surprise if I tell thee. Now, just bide thy time, and thee shall soon know."

"Do hurry, Father. I can't wait to see the surprise," cried Melissa Louisa. Her braids flew up and thumped the top of her head as she gave an extra bounce or two.

Father made the horse go like the wind. How they flew!

When they reached home, Father lifted Melissa Louisa down. He hitched the horse to the elm tree. He took his daughter's hand, and they went into the house.

There was Grandmother Gray in the kitchen. But Father said, "No, Grandmother Gray is not the surprise," and he kept tight hold of Melissa Louisa's hand. He led her straight into Mother's bedroom.

Mother was lying in the big feather bed.

Father drew Melissa Louisa near, and pulled down the covers.

"Oh-h-h-h-h!" whispered Melissa Louisa. "A *baby!* Is it ours?"

"Yes," said Mother, smiling, "it is ours."

Father led Melissa Louisa around to the other side of the bed, and folded back the covers.

"Oh-h-h-h-h-h-h-h!" whispered Melissa Louisa. Her eyes grew rounder and rounder. She stood on tiptoe and peeped over to the other side of the bed, where she had been a moment ago. On *that* side there was a baby, and on *this* side there was a baby! They were just alike.

"Father! Mother!" she cried, with her eyes almost popping out. "Are there *two* babies?"

"Yes," said Father, "twin girls!"

"Two twins!" gasped Melissa Louisa. It was hard to believe. "May we keep them both, Mother, really and truly? Nobody will come and take them away?"

"No, child," answered Mother, softly, "the Lord has given them to us, to love and to cherish."

Melissa Louisa hung over the bed, trembling with wonder and delight. "Oh, Mother, they are the most beautiful babies that ever were born. I've been asking the Lord to send us a baby for a long time, Father. But I didn't know that He would be so—oh, so *good* about it!"

"The next thing will be finding names for them," said Father.

"Yes," agreed Mother, "we shall all have to be thinking up some nice names for our twin girls."

"Names!" echoed Melissa Louisa. She stared

at her father and mother. Her heart began to thump faster than ever.

"Oh, Mother," she cried, "may I name the babies? Please, Father, let me. All by myself!"

Father and Mother smiled at each other. "If thee will choose suitable names, thee may," said Mother. "And remember that twins are generally given names that are somewhat alike."

"Wait a minute, please," said Melissa Louisa.

She dashed from the room, and out of the house. She stood under the big lilac bush, with her

fingers over her eyes, thinking very, very hard. Now or never—which should it be?

Why, of course, there was only one answer!

Melissa Louisa prayed a little prayer. "Dear Lord, let Mother and Father like the names I choose. Amen."

She ran back into the bedroom. Yes, the babies were still there, tiny and adorable. Melissa Louisa looked quite pale as she stood by the bed. She took a long breath.

"It didn't take me long to decide," she gasped. "Because, oh, Mother! Oh, Father! I want to give the babies two of *my* names. I want to name them Amanda and Miranda! Don't you see—they're the suitablest names, 'cause they're alike, just like the twins are alike. Oh, Mother! Oh, Father! Please!" Melissa Louisa clasped her hands, and looked from one to the other of her parents.

Father rubbed his chin, thinking. "What does thee say, Mother?" he asked.

"No doubt it would please their Aunt Amanda

and Aunt Miranda," murmured Mother. "But, child, doesn't thee mind giving up part of thy own name?"

"Oh, NO, Mother, I'd love to!" cried Melissa Louisa. "I have plenty of names left, all that I shall need forever and ever! And everyone will be happy. Aunt Amanda and Aunt Miranda will be happy. And Aunt Cynthia's and Aunt Jane's feelings won't be hurt. And I won't have to make the sampler!" Melissa Louisa was quite out of breath.

"I don't know what thee is talking about, child, I'm sure," said Mother. "Better calm thyself. We shall name the twins Amanda and Miranda."

"Then that's settled," said Father.

"Yes, that's settled," said Melissa Louisa, and she hopped softly about the room on one foot, full of the greatest joy.

Just then they heard Uncle Mark coming into the house.

Melissa Louisa ran out to meet him. She wanted to be the first to tell him the wonderful and surprising news that now, just since yesterday, she had twin sisters.

When Uncle Mark saw his niece flying toward him, he took a great, deep breath as if he were getting ready to run a race. His cheeks puffed out like fat, red apples. Then the words came tumbling out. "Good-day-to-thee, Melissa-Louisa-Aman-"

But he got no further, because Melissa Louisa cried out, "Stop! Stop, Uncle Mark!"

And she ran over to him and pulled him down, and clapped her hand over his mouth.

"Thee can't say that any more, Uncle Mark. Never, never any more! I gave away 'Amanda' and 'Miranda'—both of them. Just come and see who has my names now," and she led Uncle Mark proudly into the bedroom.

"See?" she said, pointing. "*There* is Amanda. And *there* is Miranda—two twins!"

No one could have been more surprised than Uncle Mark. "Whew!" he whistled. "Now, whoever heard of the like?" He turned and looked at

Melissa Louisa.

"It's too bad I can't tease thee any more. But I think it's pretty nice of thee to give the new babies part of thy name."

"Well," said Melissa Louisa, "I would have minded giving away 'Amanda' and 'Miranda' to strangers. But I was glad to give them to my own dear sisters—thee doesn't know how glad!

"So it wasn't so 'speshly nice of me, 'cause I've been wanting to give *something* away for a long time. But, anyhow, I gave them the prettiest names I had, and—'The Lord loveth a cheerful giver.' That's what the Bible says. And I do feel very cheerful, Uncle Mark."

"Goodness, child!" said Mother, and a little worry frown puckered her forehead. "She's been saying the strangest things, Mark. This has all been too exciting for her. Come here, child. Let's see if thee is a little feverish."

But Uncle Mark tossed Melissa Louisa up in his arms. He threw back his head and laughed. He

59

laughed so loud that Grandmother Gray came hurrying in from the kitchen.

"Sh-sh-sh! Mark! Thee will frighten the twins out of their wits with thy great laughter."

Uncle Mark stopped laughing until there was nothing left but chuckles and grins. And he said, "Come, thee little cheerful giver, let's go outdoors and celebrate."

He stood Melissa Louisa up on a chair, and he turned his back to her. She put her arms around his neck. He tucked her feet under his elbows, and away he galloped out of the house.

All over the yard, through the barn lot, galloped Uncle Mark, with Melissa Louisa on his back. He pranced. He cavorted. He snorted. He shied and he bucked. He whinnied and he squealed.

Melissa Louisa laughed and laughed. She laughed until her arms grew weak and she could not hold tight to Uncle Mark any longer. She slipped down and down, until at last she slipped off, and tumbled into a pile of leaves.

60

It was a jolly celebration.

CHAPTER VIII

The next day Melissa Louisa went to school. It was the first day. She could scarcely bear to leave the little Amanda, and the little Miranda. She flew back twice to kiss their downy heads. Yet she was eager to see the new teacher, too, and for school to take up.

The new teacher read a chapter from the Bible.

Then he said, "We shall now call the roll. Every one will please stand up, each one in turn, and tell me his or her full name."

Melissa Louisa's heart began to beat like a little trip-hammer. She was the very first one the teacher called upon. She stood up by her desk, and spoke in a clear, proud, and happy little voice.

"I don't have as many names as I used to have," she said, "'cause now we have twins at our house. My full name is Melissa Louisa Am—Cynthia Jane Farlow."

And this time not a single scholar laughed!

Melissa Louisa felt so happy that it seemed as if she must burst.

"School is going to be nice," she whispered to herself, "very, VERY nice!"

After school Melissa Louisa hurried home as fast as she could. She was quite out of breath when she arrived.

"Oh, Mother," she cried, "I *like* school!"

There were the babies, side by side, in Melissa

Louisa's old cradle.

She hung over them, loving them with all her heart.

"Oh, my dear twin sisters Amanda and Miranda," whispered Melissa Louisa, "you came just in the nick of time!"

THE END